THE HOKEY-POKEY MAN

Steven Kroll

illustrated by **Deborah Kogan Ray**

HOLIDAY HOUSE / NEW YORK

For sweetest Abigail
S. K.

To ice-cream lovin' kids
D. K. R.

It was the summer of 1904. Ben and Sarah lived in a tiny apartment on the Lower East Side of New York City.

They lived with their parents. And Grandma Bessie. And their older brother Aaron and older sister Rachel. Just recently, Aunt Bertha and Uncle Meyer had come from Europe. They were living in the apartment, too.

Every afternoon, when Ben and Sarah had finished their chores, they dashed downstairs to the street. The street was as crowded as their apartment. There were shops and rows of pushcarts filled with everything from fruit and vegetables to bread and fish and clothes. Peddlers shouted "Sour pickles!" "Hot pretzels!" "Fancy buttons!"

Ben and Sarah had made friends with many of the peddlers, but their favorite was Joe, The Hokey-Pokey Man. He stood on their corner with his cart, selling hokey-pokey in paper cups. Hokey-pokey was ice cream.

One day, when Ben and Sarah came to buy ice cream, Joe had a sparkle in his eye and a smile on his face.

"Children," he said, "I have a wonderful story for you."

"But you always have wonderful stories," said Ben.

"This story is better than wonderful," said Joe. "I heard it from my cousin."

Ben and Sarah sat down on the stoop.

"St. Louis," Joe began, "it is a city in the middle of this country. You know about St. Louis?"

"Yes," said Ben, "from school."

"Well, my cousin Ernest—like me, he was born in Damascus —he lives in St. Louis. Right now they are having a very big party, what they call a World's Fair, and my cousin Ernest, he went to work there selling a pastry called *zalabia*. This is a very good pastry baked on a flat waffle iron and served with sugar."

"Yum, yum," said Sarah, licking her lips.

"Wait," said Joe, "you must hear the story. Ernest was selling his *zalabia*, and near his stand, another man was selling hokey-pokey. One day, late in the afternoon, the hokey-pokey man, he ran out of paper dishes."

"How could he sell ice cream without dishes?" asked Sarah.

"He couldn't," said Joe. "So my cousin Ernest, he rolled one of his *zalabia* pastries into a cone shape, and he let it cool. Then he put a scoop of ice cream right on top. He had invented an ice-cream cone! They called it the 'World's Fair Cornucopia,' and they are selling lots of them right now!"

"Really?" said Ben.

"Do you think we could get ice-cream cones in New York?" asked Sarah.

"That is the best part of the story," said Joe. "Ernest is coming to New York with ice-cream cones. He is going to help me, and we will make big business!"

"Hooray!" shouted Sarah and Ben together.

"But remember," said Joe, "you must keep what I have told you a secret. If you do not, someone else will try to sell ice-cream cones before me."

All the way home, Ben and Sarah talked about the ice-cream cones.

By the time they reached their apartment, they were ready to burst with Joe's news. They *had* to tell somebody. Grandma Bessie was napping in her favorite chair. Aaron was the only other person home. Ben and Sarah pushed him into a corner and told him everything.

When they had finished, Aaron said, "Ice-cream cones? Ridiculous."

"What do you mean?" said Ben.

"Joe's made the whole thing up."

Ben and Sarah looked at each other. How could Aaron say that? Joe was the most honest, special person they knew.

Grandma Bessie wasn't quite asleep. She overheard part of Ben and Sarah's story.

She picked herself up and hurried across the hall to her best friend's. "Sally," she said, "I want to tell you about a new way of eating ice cream. On top of cones."

When Bessie had finished, Sally told her husband Sam, the baker. Sam smiled. "We'll try making them tonight."

On their way to the bakery, Sam and Sally ran into Simon,
the vegetable man. They told him all about the ice-cream cones.
"They sound wonderful!" said Simon.

He started home. On the way, he ran into Mario, the pretzel man. "Mario," he said, "listen to this!"

When Mario had finished listening, he, too, started dreaming about ice-cream cones.

The next afternoon, Ben and Sarah heard shouts from the street. They rushed downstairs to see what was going on.

In front of Sam's bakery, people were jumping on round balls of pastry. Scoops of ice cream were plopped on the ground.

"Hard as rocks!" said someone.

"The ice cream fell right off!" said someone else.

Inside, Sarah heard Sam say, "I couldn't make cones. I thought, why not round? They got a little hard . . ."

Down the street, people were waving their arms in front of Simon, the vegetable man's, pushcart.

"Yuck!" shouted someone. "Ice cream on a carrot tastes terrible!"

Next to Simon, Mario, the pretzel man, was having the same problem.

"Ick!" shouted someone else. "Ice cream on a pretzel is too salty!"

Louder than the rest, Mario shouted, "Whose idea was this, anyway?"

Mario, Simon, Sam, and Sally traced it back. To Grandma Bessie. To Ben and Sarah!

All eyes turned.

"It was Joe's idea!" Sarah shouted.

"He'll make it work, too," said Ben. "His cousin will help him."

"Yeah, sure," said Mario. "I bet Joe doesn't even have a cousin. He's always by himself."

"He's not even here today," said Simon.

Ben and Sarah rushed to Joe's corner. Joe wasn't there.

They walked home slowly. That night they talked to their parents about what had happened.

"You shouldn't have told Joe's secret," said their father.

"But it's good that you believe in him," said their mother. She hugged them both.

The next day, Ben and Sarah went back to Joe's corner. He wasn't there. A week passed, and still, he didn't show up.

"Maybe he went to St. Louis," said Sarah.

"He'll be back," said Ben.

Sure enough, the following afternoon, Ben and Sarah saw a long line forming on their block. It stretched on and on, up and down and around the Lower East Side.

Ben and Sarah followed the line. It led right to Joe's corner — and to Joe.

He was smiling, and so was the man beside him. At one end of his cart was a basket filled with ice-cream cones.

"I am so glad you are here!" said Joe. "I want you to meet my cousin Ernest, and I want you to have ice-cream cones free!"

Ben had vanilla. Sarah had chocolate.

"We knew you'd do it!" said Ben.

"Of course," said Joe. "Didn't I tell you I would?"

By then a crowd had gathered around Joe's cart. There were Sally and Sam and Aaron. There were Mario and Simon and even Grandma Bessie.

"You were right!" they said to Ben and Sarah. "Joe's the greatest!"

"Three cheers for Joe!" said Mario.

"Hooray for the ice-cream cone!" said Aaron.

And the whole crowd shouted "Hooray!"

Sure enough, the following afternoon, Ben and Sarah saw a long line forming on their block. It stretched on and on, up and down and around the Lower East Side.

Ben and Sarah followed the line. It led right to Joe's corner — and to Joe.

He was smiling, and so was the man beside him. At one end of his cart was a basket filled with ice-cream cones.

"I am so glad you are here!" said Joe. "I want you to meet my cousin Ernest, and I want you to have ice-cream cones free!"

AUTHOR'S NOTE

The International Association of Ice Cream Manufacturers gives credit for the invention of the ice-cream cone to Ernest A. Hamwi at the 1904 St. Louis World's Fair. I have used that version as the basis for my story, but it is not the only one. A patent for a cone mold was issued to Italo Marchiony before the Fair opened. Later, at least two other contenders, David Avayou and Abe Doumar, appeared. Both claimed to have invented the ice-cream cone at the St. Louis World's Fair. Avayou said he got the idea from France, where ice cream was eaten from *paper* cones. Doumar told a story similar to Ernest Hamwi's. Who really gets the credit is anybody's guess.

Text copyright © 1989 by Steven Kroll
Illustrations copyright © 1989 by Deborah Kogan
All rights reserved
Printed in the United States of America
First Edition

LIBRARY OF CONGRESS
Library of Congress Cataloging-in-Publication Data

Kroll, Steven.
The hokey-pokey man / written by Steven Kroll ;
illustrated by Deborah Kogan Ray.
p.   cm.
Summary: Hearing about the invention of the ice cream
cone at the 1904 World's Fair, an ice cream peddler
hopes to be the first to
introduce the idea in New York City.
ISBN 0-8234-0728-4
[1. Ice cream, ices, etc.—Fiction.
2. New York (N.Y.)—Fiction.]
I. Ray, Deborah Kogan, 1940-   ill.   II. Title.
PZ7.K9225Ho 1989
[E]—dc19   88-17012   CIP   AC

ISBN 0-8234-0728-4